TERRY'S CREW

By TERRY CREWS
and CORY THOMAS

Little, Brown and Company
New York Boston

About This Book

This book was edited by Andrea Colvin and designed by Megan McLaughlin. The production was supervised by Bernadette Flinn, and the production editor was Lindsay Walter-Greaney. The text was set in Collect Em Now BB and Mikado.

Little, Brown and Company
Hachette Book Group
1290 Avenue of the Americas, New York, NY 10104
Visit us at LBYR.com

First Edition: November 2022

Little, Brown and Company is a division of Hachette Book Group, Inc. The Little, Brown name and logo are trademarks of Hachette Book Group, Inc.

The publisher is not responsible for websites (or their content) that are not owned by the publisher.

Library of Congress Cataloging-in-Publication Data
Names: Crews, Terry, 1968– author. | Thomas, Cory, illustrator.
Title: Terry's crew / by Terry Crews and Cory Thomas.
Description: First edition. | New York : Little, Brown and Company, 2022. | Summary: "Inquisitive young artist Terry strives to make space for himself as the new kid at Rock City Academy, a place where he can finally hone his talents. Terry learns the consequences of dreaming big and the value of real friends along the way"—Provided by publisher.
Identifiers: LCCN 2021050369 | ISBN 9780316499965 (hardcover) | ISBN 9780316499958 (ebook)
Subjects: CYAC: Artists–Fiction. | Schools–Fiction. | Friendship–Fiction.
Classification: LCC PZ7.1.C7436 Te 2022 | DDC [Fic]–dc23
LC record available at https://lccn.loc.gov/2021050369

ISBNs: 978-0-316-49996-5 (hardcover), 978-0-316-49998-9 (paperback), 978-0-316-49995-8 (ebook), 978-0-316-27341-1 (ebook), 978-0-316-27586-6 (ebook)

PRINTED IN CANADA

TC

Hardcover: 10 9 8 7 6 5 4 3 2 1

Paperback: 10 9 8 7 6 5 4 3 2 1

To my high school art teacher, Dwight Eichelberg...for believing in me when I didn't believe in myself —TC

4

6

8

Here, pry it open with this.

Hey, little dude, we're gonna get you outta here real soon.

You're going on to bigger things.

POP!

I know we didn't raise disrespectful sons who run into this house and don't say hi, did we, Tonya?

I'm pretty sure we didn't--

but maybe this son is excited about starting a new school tomorrow.

Sorry. Hi, everybody!

Much better.

Hey, everyone.

CREEEAK!

About time! I almost left your plate for you in front of a locked door.

Dinner smells good, Troy.

You better believe dinner tastes good, too.

After a really good dinner.

I'm really sorry about today. I shouldn't have told anyone about what happened.

≑Sigh≑
...I mean, maybe they're right about me being slow.

Somebody smart would know not to say anything.

It's fine... We all make mistakes.

Mom keeps believing Dad is gonna fix the hole by the stairs.

Besides, half our family saw what happened. So it probably would've leaked anyw--*≑sigh≑*

Wow, that was a lot from them today.

Hey, I thought you were in a rush.

I mean, I am.

Just worried about those kids spreading stupid stories.

What happens if someone from my new school hears them?

30

38

OK, Phase 3A of the Big Dream Plan is in motion!

What's that, Terry? Do you know the answer?

Uh, yeah. The stratosphere.

Good job!

I love it here!

Terry! Just the young man I want to see.

Hey, Mr. Montgomery.

So, I was watching you in PE class the other day, and I've gotta say...

...you're wasting your talents with this doodling when you can run like that.

I don't think so. I'm pretty sure I can do everything I put my mind to.

I'm gonna be a multihyphenate.

Multihyph-- OK, that's the kinda spunk I like to see!

But a kid like you...Well, I have an idea.

43

All kinds of ideas later.

What's the big rush?

I've gotta show Mom Phase 4 of my Big Dream Plan!

The Academy is having a Talent Show and I'm going to enter!

Like, on stage? Are you sure about that? If you need my help--

I think you need to be an Academy student.

I'm definitely not that.

Well, you don't need to be an Academy student to help with this lawn. So, c'mon.

And, Terry, you hurry up back out here, too.

But Phase 4... ≈Sigh≈

Wow!

So good!

OK, class dismissed, I guess. Don't forget about your essays next week!

Thanks, guys!

Nice sketches, Terry.

I never introduced myself. I'm Rick.

You're gonna join my Talent Show team, right?

We need someone to design our costumes.

I'm in!

Cool! Let's meet up behind the library after school to talk about it.

After school. Talking about it.

So, look, Terry. I'm glad you want to join our team...

...but we need to know for sure that you're cool.

A lot of people want to join us, since we won last year.

How do I prove I'm cool?

That kid.

Go over and knock that math book out of his hands.

Dude is always reading stuff that isn't even assigned.

Such a loser.

48

51

Home.

Troy! Why are you waiting for me?

More rat traps?

Nope. Thought we could walk to the comic store and see what new comics they have.

Let's go!

I see you couldn't wait to get away from those fancy kids.

Well, it's been kinda hard making friends.

Yeah, I heard you and Mom talking about that stuff the other day.

Nooo!

I think I might have made a new friend today, actually.

But it was kinda weird how.

Need me to beat anyone up?

56

"Last year, Rick and I were the new kids.

"We'd always hang out after school, talking about Harry Wizard.

"He wanted to start a school paper.

"But then Mr. Montgomery got ahold of him after PE class one day.

"The next thing I knew, he wanted to join the football team.

"And that was it.

"A few months later, he was Rick Duval: Most Popular Guy at Academy.

"Just because he won a few games.

"Ugh. That's why I don't like sports people."

Well, they aren't all the same, you know.

Fine, but here you are, also a sports person and also being a jerk!

Wake up, Terry!

Xander is over there. Are you gonna say anything?

Huh? Yeah, I am.

He shouldn't have to suffer just for my Big Dream Plan.

Your Big Who What?

It's something I've been working on for a while.

Kids in my neighborhood did to me kind of what I did to Xander.

And I remember how that made me feel.

Can we maybe talk about this at lunch?

Perhaps. But only if Xander is OK.

≶Sigh≶ Just get it over with.

I'm not here to knock your things over again.

Just wanted to say I'm sorry.

Really sorry. That's not even who I am.

Lunchtime.

Where've you been, Terry? I gotta run my costume ideas past you.

...Um, yeah. I, uh...

Just spit it out.

Um, thanks for asking me to be in your group, but I have to, uh, decline.

What? Why? Because of yesterday?

I'm sure Xander's over it, and Rani...

Well, Rani is always mad about something.

Xander's over it because I apologized.

You should think about it yourself.

I'd rather make friends who don't bully people. Or ask me to.

68

74

Is this yours?

My brother dreams about buying cool bikes, but this is so much cooler!

Sheesh, Terry, you've never ridden in a golf cart?

We're supposed to share these with the other residents in this community.

But I keep this one just for me.

So awesome!

Sorry, guys, I didn't mean to make things awkward.

Well...

I honestly just thought Rani didn't like me, like a lot of people at school.

What? No. Why would I not like you?

Before the whole "Terry bullying me" thing, you'd always walk right past me.

Well, it's just that sometimes I can be too intense, and people end up getting mad at me.

Next day. Bleh.

What's up, li'l man?

Haven't seen you in a minute. How's Rich Kid Academy?

Hey, Emilio.

It started off rough, then got really great, then my friends and I entered the Talent Show.

But now it's rough again because my mom is worried that all the awesomeness is bringing down my grades.

Grades are always a bummer.

If you wanna make angry noises, I have a new drum kit at the crib.

Figure we can come up with a plan for you or at least jam out for a little bit.

OK!

OK, we've gotta figure this out soon so you can head on home.

Don't want your mom any more upset.

Blah.

So, I'm thinking: She said you can't compete, but...

...she didn't say anything about being the host.

Huh? Why host?

You're spending too much time practicing for the show, right?

But as a host, you could still be part of the whole thing, and it wouldn't take up anywhere as much time.

A little bending the rules never hurt nobody.

Wait! What about my friends?

Good point. No idea.

I know! They can help set up an awesome stage.

Rani could build stuff, Xander could organize the program, and I could paint some kind of mural.

The crew can be a stage crew.

Now that's a plan!

OK, get outta here before your folks get mad.

I have big boy stuff to do now anyway.

What kind of stuff?

Stuff I'll tell you about when you're older.

Trust me. You don't need to know everything.

Says you.

The next day.

Ms. Randall, has anyone asked to host the Talent Show?

Usually, it goes to whichever teacher lost the coin toss.

No student has ever asked. It's honestly a pretty boring gig.

Sweet! So--can I do it?

And can Rani and Xander help?

Sorry, sir. Just mad.

I get it. I know how hard that is for you to control.

The fact is now it seems you have a little competition and, well, competition breeds strength and character.

Furthermore--

there aren't many people who look like you and Terry at the Academy.

If you ask me, y'all should stick together.

Yo! Are you Rick Duval?

Can't be. Why's an all-star athlete hanging out here?

Yeah, you all must have seen me in the newspaper. Or maybe one of you has a TV?

Man, when you threw that Hail Mary and won the state championship, my whole family was cheering.

Yeah, man, you repping Rock City well. What brings you here?

You looking for Emilio?

Well, there's this new kid at my school who lives around here.

He may be trying out for the team soon.

I wanted to find out more about Terry before making any real decisions.

Ha, oh man. You mean Trickle Down?! That dude can barely walk without tripping.

Among *other things* he can't control.

What other things?

105

That happened a long time ago.

Heh, doesn't matter.

If you don't want the whole school to find out, you'll drop out from hosting the Talent Show.

From what I've heard, they shouldn't let you near a stage anyway.

...Oh no...

I'll give you some time to think about it. Meet me after school.

"At my aunt Tyra's wedding reception--

"I was supposed to recite a poem, but then I got up on stage and...

Yes?

I forgot the words.

How embarrassing.

There's more.

"I ran offstage without paying attention and knocked over their giant wedding cake.

"Sweet Aunt Tyra rushes over to comfort me, twists her ankle on the icing, and falls on the floor, howling like an old ghost.

"...I...make a mess down the front of my tuxedo."

"Now everybody in the place is looking at me and the mess I made, and...

Rick pushed you into it. I understand.

My grandpa is always pushing me into things.

"Gotta carry on the Vanclief legacy."

I wanna be more than just rich.

And I just wanna hang out with friends.

My parents are so strict and worried about me getting hurt.

Most weekends, I'm staring out of my bedroom window.

All because of your sister?

≈Sigh≈ Yeah.

My sister is a lot older than I am.

When I was younger, she got really sick and stayed in the hospital for a long time.

I can barely remember things, but she almost died.

My parents changed after she got better.

They barely let us leave the house.

So you get sick when you go outside?

Nope. It's definitely not that kind of sickness.

My dad's a doctor, so you'd think he'd know better.

116

Leaving
Rock City.

Probably
going to get
in a lot of
trouble for
this.

But it's
totally
worth it.

Thank y'all very much for the tour.

I'll never understand art, but maybe Terry got something out of it.

 Some people just don't have the depth.

 Little Terry most certainly does, I see.

Maybe one day we'll be sharing *your* obscenely priced art on these walls.

Bet on it.

 Bet on me!

 All right, all right, let's get going. You need to get back to where you belong.

122

Bro! It's late!

Mom and Dad had me looking for you. They're real upset.

A letter came in today about you hosting the Talent Show?

Whatever. This day can't get any worse.

I'll tell you about it later.

Hey, Mom and Dad.

Come sit down, Terry.

We have to ask about this letter.

You promised your mother you wouldn't be participating in this Talent Show.

Well, I just thought that hosting was different.

I'm not participating, just helping out.

Looks like your real talent is finding loopholes.

I'm sorry. I just really wanted to do something different and fun.

You should have asked us first at least.

But all you guys ever say yes to is schoolwork.

And chores.

And, like...

...fiscal responsibility.

You gotta understand that you won't get handed many chances.

Rock City Academy is a big chance.

From there you can go on to bigger places than you dream of.

Or you could just stay here and work with me at the repair shop.

Since you wanna get B-minuses and stuff.

But Xander and Rani don't get perfect grades and no one's banning them from the show.

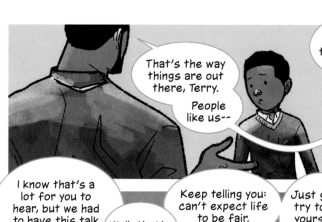

That's the way things are out there, Terry.

People like us--

we have to be exceptional at every turn to get even half as far as we should.

No slipups.

I know that's a lot for you to hear, but we had to have this talk sooner or later.

Well, that's not fair.

Keep telling you: can't expect life to be fair.

Just gotta try to live yours the best way you can.

Yeah.

Your dad thinks we should let you host the Talent Show.

I can't promise I'll be there to watch.

But--

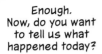
Enough. Now, do you want to tell us what happened today?

My guidance counselor, Mr. Montgomery, asked me to meet him at this gallery show thing in Diamond Vale.

It just... wasn't as fun as I expected.

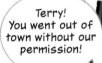
Terry! You went out of town without our permission!

With a man we don't know?!

I'm gonna have to meet this Mr. Montgomery and ask him if he's lost his foolish mind!

OK. Fine. Can I just go to bed?

Feels like there's more to all this, but we can talk later.

You okay, bro?

Maybe tomorrow, Troy.

130

140

OK, OK. We get the hint.

Let's get outta here, Montgomery, and let these kids do their thing.

Bye.

OK, spill it.

Why are you mad at Mr. M?

It's a long story, but I'll tell you what.

He's gonna eat his words.

That's a disturbing metaphor if you think about it.

I'm gonna crush the Talent Show and win the Super Bowl and land on Venus just to prove him wrong.

Then you'd better start by acing your geometry test tomorrow.

I'm gonna ace every test from now on until I'm president of every college!

Three days left.

I don't know what this is, Adrian, but I love it.

Hey, Ms. Randall, need any help?

Oh, fantastic. Yes, I do. Thanks, Rick.

I guess I'm here at the perfect time.

CLANG-A-LANG

What was that?

156

157

Break a leg, Terry.

Thanks, Troy!

Sheesh! You're finally here.

Relax. I'm two hours early.

Two hours early is late.

Much bigger.

But we have bigger problems than that.

Ms. Randall can't find your costume!

Oh no...

For what? You're not hosting the show.

Or do I tell the Legend of Trickle Down?

I mean, I haven't even told my friends here.

That doesn't even make sense, Rick.

How would there even be a show with no host?

I dunno. Maybe I'll just do it, then.

My guys are ready to drop out if I do. They follow my lead. Ain't that right, guys?

See? They love it.

So, what's it going to be, Terry?

Is that why you stopped hanging out with me?

Because I'm not some competitive meathead?

No, not exactly. It's just that...

...You know what? I'm done with this.

Mr. Montgomery says competition breeds strength, and he's right.

What if he's not, Rick?

What if building bonds makes you stronger than fighting?

Sounds like somebody who's scared to fight.

He gets way too involved with you kids, thinking he's helping, but instead--

He says a bunch of ignorant stuff?

Rani, don't be rude.

Even if you're right.

But, you kids didn't hear that from me.

Hear what? We never listen to adults.

Competition was a little too much for you, Rick?

Mr. Montgomery,

I did my best.

You think losing is your best?

I...

All right, guys, seeing Mr. M get owned was worth keeping my parents waiting.

But I've gotta go before they freak out.

My grandpa hates sitting in one place if it isn't making him any money.

Me too.

The hustle never stops.

The what?

They seem OK for some rich kids.

You oughta hang out. We're a crew now!

Y'all ready to go?

Yeah, I'm beat.

Hey, li'l man! Good job!

Emilio! You came!

Did you see me do your hosting idea?

Nah, that was all you, man.

That's a wicked hat, by the way!

Ha, forgot I was still wearing it.

I was gonna watch you wear that forever.

Terry's Crew is a fictionalized version of my life. I grew up in Flint, Michigan, which is a *lot* like Rock City. Flint was changing very quickly in my early teens, as the auto industry, which provided the ways and means for most of its citizens, began to slowly fade away. But while that happened, my dreams kept getting bigger and bigger, and I was fortunate enough to attend a special school that encouraged all my talents—from art and dance all the way to science and sports. Most of the time I was asked to choose the one I liked best, but it was like choosing a favorite immediate family member: Each one held a special place in my heart.

I really did have an older streetwise friend like Emilio, who always looked out for me, encouraged me, and believed in me. I also loved to draw and paint, and having that outlet always fed an imaginative cycle where art was a pipeline to even more ideas—every one of which I wanted to see realized. I even really hosted my high school talent show, the precursor to hosting *America's Got Talent*—the biggest talent show in the world!

I also encountered great and supportive friends like Rani and Xander who I could trust to tell me the truth about my ideas and, more important, myself. What I loved about my school was that Black or white, rich or poor, artistic or athletic, we all contributed to one another's goals and dreams. Like Emilio would say, "You'll be whoever you let yourself be." My own Rock City Academy was where you were allowed to "let yourself be."

Now, that doesn't mean I didn't have obstacles. Most of the time I had to get out of my own way instead of trying to be cool by joking at others' expense or taking the bait of competing with others when I should have been creating with them. That always ended in disappointment. My parents were *very* strict, but in hindsight they just wanted to keep me out of the trouble plenty of my peers were getting into at the time...although it took me years to understand that. I also had some teachers who meant well but ended up not supporting me in the best way, like the professor who really did tell me I wasn't good enough to achieve my dreams. I may not have been good enough at the time, but I learned that most skills can be developed and achieved through hard work and patience. I found out things are not "you either have it or you don't," but rather "you can have it when it's earned," especially if you get good feedback from a great crew.

When I set out to write a book for young readers, I wanted to use my own experiences to share some of the lessons I've learned along the way (like Dream Big! Have a Crew!) and hopefully inspire those readers to keep going, even when things don't feel like they are working out.

Love,

Terry

TERRY CREWS

Favorite Subject: Art
Favorite Book: *Cara Cloudjumper:*
The Antiverse Saga
Favorite Animal: Panther chameleon
Hobbies: Everything
Big Dream: Being a multihyphenate

XANDER VANCLIEF

Favorite Subject: Algebra II
Favorite Book: *To Kill a Mockingbird*
Favorite Animal: Keel-billed toucan
Hobbies: Photography and reading
about photography and reading
Big Dream: ???
(Whatever Grandpa wants)

RICK DUVAL

Favorite Subject: P.E.
Favorite Book: That one about pirates that we watched in homeroom on TV
Favorite Animal: Sharks
Hobbies: Competition
Big Dream: Winning

I would like to thank my wife, Rebecca; my children, Naomi, Azriel, Tera, Wynfrey, and Isaiah; my granddaughter, Miley; my parents, Terry and Patricia Crews; my brother, Marcelle; and my sister, Micki.

Thanks also to my teacher Dwight Eichelberg and coach Lee Williams; to my agent, Albert Lee; manager, Troy Zien; and attorney, David Krintzman.

And finally, to my editor, Andrea Colvin, and this book's illustrator, Cory Thomas.

— TC

I want to thank my wife—the Dharma to my Greg (which is apparently a different show to *Will & Grace*). Throughout the long hours, sleepless nights, and hair loss, she has shown me so much love and encouragement. More than this book, I couldn't do life so fully without her. Thank you, Banakayi.

And to everyone who fed into me, supported me, guided me, and mocked my imposter syndrome—thank you, too. Ashelyn and Marlene and everyone who made me believe this could be a thing. You were right.

— CT

CORY THOMAS is a Trinidad-born illustrator, writer, and interesting man. In 2005, he began the newspaper comic strip *Watch Your Head*, and in 2013 began his journey into children's literature. Cory now lives in Atlanta, Georgia, with his wife, Netflix, and too many hats. He invites you to visit him at seethomas.com.

TERRY CREWS can be described in a lot of ways: author, action-movie hero, sitcom star, TV host, children's book illustrator, advertising pitchman, playable video game character, high-end furniture designer, and human rights activist. Crews is best known for his breakout roles on *Brooklyn Nine-Nine* and *Everybody Hates Chris*, hosting *America's Got Talent*, and his voicework in the animated films *Cloudy with a Chance of Meatballs 2* and *The Willoughbys*. *Terry's Crew* is his debut middle-grade graphic novel.